THE END

CATS RULE!

DOGS DROOL

BY **JOHN BRAY** ILLUSTRATED BY **JOSH CLELAND**

STARRY FOREST BOOKS

First edition 2022

Library of Congress Catalog Card Number 2022933018
ISBN 978-1-951784-12-6 (picture book)
ISBN 978-1-951784-89-8 (ebook)
Manufactured in China
Lot #: 2 4 6 8 10 9 7 5 3 1
05/22

STARRY
FOREST
BOOKS

Starry Forest Books, Inc.
P.O. Box 1797
217 East 70th Street
New York, NY 10021

starryforestbooks.com | @starryforestbks

For Lennon,
who's always beginning.
— **J. B**.

Dedicated to my nephew, Liam,
and nieces, Taylor, Brynn,
and Blair. May your endings
lead to fantastic beginnings.
— **J. C.**

What? It is! Oh. You're probably confused because this book is just beginning.

But it's still **THE END**.

Maybe you were getting dressed and decided to read instead because reading is more fun than finding matching socks. That's **THE END** of searching for socks.

Maybe you just finished eating lunch.
That's **THE END** of lunch.

But don't worry. There's still dinner.
And sometimes dessert.

If you were outside adventuring
and it started raining,

that's **THE END** of adventuring.

Or you might not be at **THE END**
of anything.

But you're definitely not at the beginning either.

Maybe you're building a fort.

That means you're in the middle—

the place where beginnings
and endings meet.

If you run out of blankets,
the middle could feel short.

If you keep building and building, it might feel long.

DINO CAVE
ENTER

But you can't be in the middle forever.
That gets boring.

Boredom is **THE END** of fun.

Which means that it's time to begin something new.

When you do something—like read this book

or go on an adventure—

something else—like finding socks

or eating lunch—is ending.

That something could be better than what you were doing.

Or it could be worse.

THE END might be a big deal.

Or you might not
even notice it.

But **THE END** of one thing

is the beginning of something else.

And the beginning of one thing is
THE END of another.

And that's okay.

THE BEGINNING

Of what? Well, that's up to you.